Tiana

Louis

STARRING

Prince
Naveen

The Frogs

Ray

First published by Parragon in 2009
Parragon
Queen Street House
4 Queen Street
Bath BA1 1HE, UK

ISBN 978-1-4075-6174-5

Printed in China

DISNEY
THE PRINCESS AND THE FROG

Bath · New York · Singapore · Hong Kong · Cologne · Delhi · Melbourne

One evening, Tiana and her friend Charlotte LaBouff were listening to Tiana's mother, Eudora, reading a story about a frog who needed a kiss from a princess to turn him into a human prince. Charlotte was ready to kiss a frog if it meant she could be a princess! But not so for Tiana! She would never kiss a frog!

Back at home, Tiana and her father, James, talked of their dream of opening their own restaurant. Later, Tiana wanted to wish on the Evening Star so their dream would come true. James encouraged her to wish, but also to remember to work hard – and never forget the importance of family and friends.

The years went by and Tiana became a beautiful young woman. Her father had passed away, but Tiana was still determined to open their restaurant. She waited tables day and night, and saved every spare penny she could. She knew that her hard work would pay off one day, and her dream would come true.

Not far away, a carefree prince arrived in town just in time for Mardi Gras. Tiana's friend Charlotte was especially excited to meet Prince Naveen at her father's masquerade ball that night. "I'm going to need about 500 of your man-catching beignets," she told Tiana.

Tiana was thrilled when Charlotte paid her enough money for Tiana to finally buy her restaurant!

That afternoon, Tiana made an offer on the old sugar mill that she and her father had picked out long ago.

"It will be the place Daddy and I always dreamed of," Tiana told her mother as she imagined how glamorous the restaurant would look when it was done.

"Your daddy may not have gotten the place he always wanted," said Eudora gently, "but he had something better. He had love. And that's all I want for you, sweetheart."

Tiana just laughed. Love was the last thing on her mind!

Meanwhile, downtown, a sinister figure approached Prince Naveen and his valet, Lawrence. Dr Facilier practiced bad voodoo – and he had wicked plans for the prince.

Lawrence didn't trust the stranger, but Naveen was intrigued and followed Facilier to a magic shop. Facilier told both men he could give them exactly what they most wanted, and used a magic talisman to cast a spell.

Later, at the masquerade ball, Charlotte waited impatiently for her prince. "Maybe I just have to wish harder," she told Tiana. Gazing up at the Evening Star, Charlotte wished for her prince to come.

Just then, Prince Naveen arrived! But it wasn't really the prince at all. Back in his dark parlour, Dr Facilier had magically transformed Lawrence so that he looked exactly like Naveen! The plan was for Lawrence to marry Charlotte, and split her fortune with Facilier.

At the ball, Tiana discovered that someone had offered more money for the sugar mill. The deal was off! Tiana was so upset, she tripped into her beignet table. Her dress was ruined, but Charlotte gave her a beautiful princess gown to wear.

After she had changed, Tiana wandered out to the balcony and looked up at the Evening Star. Feeling a little foolish, she closed her eyes and made a wish.

When Tiana opened her eyes again, a frog was staring up at her.

"I am Prince Naveen of Maldonia," the frog said. Dr Facilier had turned Prince Naveen into a frog, and Naveen thought that only a kiss from a princess could turn him back into a human. He also thought that Tiana was a princess. "Surely I could offer you some type of reward. A wish I could grant, perhaps?"

Tiana felt sorry for the frog. Plus, she really did want her restaurant. She closed her eyes and – SMOOCH!

Naveen was still a frog – but now Tiana was a frog, too!

Tiana was completely frantic. She tackled Naveen and they tumbled down to the masquerade ball. The party turned to chaos! Naveen and Tiana grabbed onto some balloons and drifted to the bayou.

That's where Naveen found out that Tiana was not a real princess.

"No wonder the kiss didn't work!" he exclaimed. But Naveen couldn't be too angry – he had lied about being rich.

Nevertheless, the two frogs would both have to work hard to find a way out of this mess!

The next morning, Naveen and Tiana met a friendly, trumpet-playing alligator named Louis. He and Naveen talked about jazz music, but all Tiana cared about was finding someone to break the spell that had turned them into frogs.

Louis told them a magic woman named Mama Odie might be able to help. He agreed to take them to her. Maybe she would turn Louis human, too, and his dream of playing in a jazz band would finally come true!

Meanwhile, Lawrence – magically disguised as Naveen – was already proposing to Charlotte! But the spell was running out quickly. Luckily, Charlotte was so thrilled at the idea of being a princess that she didn't even notice Lawrence changing back into his true self!

"We're going to have ourselves a Mardi Gras wedding!" Charlotte squealed.

Back in the bayou, Tiana and Naveen tangled tongues while trying to catch food – a firefly! The firefly, named Ray, helped them and then kindly offered to show them the way to Mama Odie's.

Once on land, some hunters captured Tiana. Naveen bravely hopped to the rescue and Tiana was able to escape. When the hunters tried to club the frogs, they hit each other instead!

Suddenly, the shadows sent by Facilier grabbed Naveen! Luckily, Mama Odie saved him.

Mama Odie was an old woman who used voodoo to help people.

"We need to be human," Tiana told her

"You want to be human, but you're blind to what you need!" Mama Odie declared.

Tiana peeked into Mama Odie's tub of gumbo and saw an image of Big Daddy LaBouff as the king of Mardi Gras – which made Charlotte a princess! If Naveen could kiss 'Princess' Charlotte before midnight, then he and Tiana would become human again!

Tiana, Naveen, Louis and Ray caught a ride on a riverboat to the city. Along the way, Naveen confessed to Ray that he was in love with Tiana!

Naveen surprised her with a romantic dinner. As they drifted along, Tiana pointed out the sugar mill she and her father had chosen for their restaurant so long ago.

Naveen's heart sank. In order to make Tiana's dream come true, he would have to marry Charlotte and beg her to buy Tiana her restaurant. There was no other way to get the money for the sugar mill in time. Heartbroken, Naveen left Tiana – and was snatched up by the evil shadows!

Back at the LaBouff estate – WHOOSH! – the shadows swept in with Naveen. Facilier was thrilled. He used Naveen to restore the talisman's magic, and Lawrence changed into the handsome prince once more. Now Lawrence could marry Charlotte.

Naveen finally understood the wicked plot – just as Facilier locked him inside a small chest.

Ray found Naveen and freed him from the chest. Just as Charlotte and her groom were about to say "I do," Naveen jumped onto Lawrence!

The frog quickly pulled the talisman from the impostor's neck and tossed it to Ray. Furious that his plan was falling apart, Facilier told Lawrence – who looked like his old self – to stay hidden.

In a different part of the parade, Louis was finally playing in a Mardi Gras jazz band! Just then Ray flew by, struggling with the heavy talisman. Facilier and the evil shadows were right behind him! Louis knew what he had to do. He turned his back on the band and took off to help Ray.

Ray found Tiana sitting in the cemetery, and gave her the talisman before flying off to fight Facilier and the shadows. But Facilier knocked down the little bug and stepped on him!

Facilier quickly caught up with Tiana. Thinking fast, she threatened to shatter the talisman, but Facilier played a trick on her. Tiana magically found herself in her dream restaurant – and she was human again!

"Perhaps I can offer you a little something," bargained Facilier.

Then the illusion changed and Tiana saw her father.

"Don't forget your poor daddy," Facilier said, reminding her of her father's dream.

"My daddy never got what he wanted," Tiana declared. Suddenly she understood everything – clear as day. "But he had what he needed." Her daddy knew that the love of his family was more important than anything else – that and the way he could cook and bring together people from all over to share food and good times.

Tiana shattered the talisman. Instantly, she was a frog again. And Facilier lost his control over the shadows. They surrounded him. Soon all that was left of Facilier was his hat.

Tiana rushed to the church. There she overheard Naveen promise to marry Charlotte if she kissed him.

"But you must give Tiana all the money she requires for her restaurant," said Naveen.

"Don't," Tiana protested, as she hopped out of the shadows. "My dream wouldn't mean anything without you."

Charlotte knew true love when she saw it. "I'll kiss you," she said to Naveen. "No marriage required!"

But it was too late. The clock chimed midnight! Tiana and Naveen didn't mind. They were in love – even if they were still frogs.

Just then Louis raced up. Crying, he held a wounded Ray. Facilier had hurt him badly. He was dying. Tiana and Naveen raced to his side. Ray was happy to see that his friends were together and in love. Then his light flickered out. Returning to the bayou, the friends bid the little firefly good-bye.

A little while later, Naveen and Tiana were married by Mama Odie in the bayou. As Naveen kissed Tiana, something truly magical happened: the frogs turned back into humans!

"Like I told you, kissing a princess breaks the spell!" Mama Odie said with a laugh.

"And once you became my wife . . . that made you –" Naveen began.

"A princess," Tiana finished. "You just kissed yourself a princess!"

Soon there was a new restaurant in town
– Tiana's Palace. It was the best place to go for
good food, lively music and fun with friends and
family.

Tiana had nothing more to wish for, because
she had everything she'd ever wanted – and
everything she needed.